Crybaby

Caroline Lewis

Contents

Chapter 1 - Monday Mornings Are A Battle

F emi

The sounds of the people in the hallways were all drowned out by my music. The calm songs helped ease my heart and escape my worries. The sweet solitude and perfect distance from my class, I could reach out my hand to their blurry figures but we'd never touch. Something I didn't want to change, it was perfect that way for me. I stopped my slow steps infront of room 43, even though I needed to go in I could feel how my feet were heavy. Shoes filled with rocks, that's how it felt so I took a deep breath and took out my headphones. Standing infront of the door forever wasn't gonna work, I'd have to go in eventually. I always needed a moment of mental preparation before entering class.

Even though the teacher never made official seats for us we all sort of claimed our spots somehow. So I'd never worried over someone taking my seat- which was at the far back on the left- since just like how I knew not to take the seat by the right row near the window- that was were Jessica would usually sit, she knew not to take mine. We all just had a mutual understanding, well of course unless someone would be a little late and leave their seat open because then another student could snatch it away. And that just happened, someone was sitting in my perfect seat with a nonchalant expression, not knowing just how special that seat was!

I bit my lower lip and looked around to see if there were anymore places I could sit, I turned to where my best friend Darianna would always sit but someone was already sitting next to her. A shaky sigh escaped my lips and my eyes went back to darting across the room.

"Femi please sit down already!"

The stern voice from my least favourite teacher, didn't even feel like thinking of her name, made me jump. All eyes were on me, well they weren't but it sure as hell felt like it! The cold sweat dripped down my neck and made me squirm.

One seat was free.

And before I knew it I was already sitting there.

I had rushed to it, I wanted to just turn tiny and act like this never happened. My body immidiately melted ontop of the table, well atleast it felt like it. No bones in my body, just fluid, I could't move a muscle and didn't want to. Monday mornings were like fighting in a war, high tension, stress and just wanting to go back home to your comfy bed. I let out yet another sigh and glanced up to see who I was sitting with.

I'd been so focused on getting a place to sit I didn't even care enough to look at who was next to the free seat. It was somewhat embarrassing actually.

My body turned to stone once I realized who I was next to, that tan skin that had a soft warmth to it, that jet black hair that fell over his eyelases and could suck you right in. The way his stormy gray eyes were focused on his phone, not once darting up to see what the teacher was writing. They were locked in place and he hadn't even noticed I was staring, or maybe he just didn't care. Either way I made sure to not make a single sound, even breathing felt dangerous. My body stayed down and angled as far away from him as possible. There wasn't much I could do when we were only inches apart but I still tried my best.

Of all the people I just had to run to where Ashton Yang was sitting, my oh-so favourite childhood bully!

To let out a sigh that would be heard throughout the whole earth was what I wanted to do the most but held back from. Especially since any noise would most likely piss off Ashton and that was something I couldn't risk.

'Monday Mornings really are a battle..'

Chapter 2 - Some Things Can't Be Known

F^{emi}

My eyes were glued in place, even though my brain was screaming at me to just look away I still couldn't. I didn't hate him, rather I feared him. Even if we were just kids those casual mockings he would give me hurt, deeply. So when he stopped out of nowhere I couldn't feel happy. Was he planning something? Did he get bored of me? Was he gonna go back to how he used to be? It was all unknown when it came to him, it wasn't like I could just go up to him and ask either so I was left with the questions on my own. Darianna had tried to give me comfort by saying that she'd beat him up if he hurt me in any way, which while I appreciated, would only of made things worse for me so it was a definate no. Back to the point, the mystery he was made me fear what the future could be when it came to him and made me not want to go near him. Even if we were in the same class I'd just avoid him any way I could.

We had different social circles and never sat near each other, I made sure of that, so for me to have blundered this badly and accidenally sit next to him of all people nearly brought me to tears. Crying infront of him would get me killed! Well emotionally. What if his interest would come back after seeing me cry and he'd go back to bullying me? There were no answers and only questions so to save myself I kept my face down the whole lesson.

Somehow the lesson ended without me dying from shock, he never once looked my way nor said anything. He didn't bother me in any way. He could've actually not realised that I was next to him, but I wasn't gonna complain about something like that.

Someone placed their hands on my shoulders and forcefully turned me around to face them. I immidietaly knew who it was just from their firm grip. Darianna Crespo, my best friend who always tried to support me in anyway she could and accepted my meek personality instead of scorning me for it. "Stop clutching on my shoulders like that, you're gonna kill me." I said with a light chuckle. She kept her grip firm and actually tightened it a bit.

"You're staying with me after school today, okay?" Her smile was bright and nearly as blinding as the sun but I wasn't gonna let her light blind me into doing something stupid.

My eyebrow raised as I eyed her closely, "why?" I didn't even bother to lift my arms to get her hands of my shoulders, my strength was nowhere near hers.

"What's with that look? It's not like I'm gonna make you vandalize the school with me."

"Then what is it?" My head cocked to the side.

She let out a loud grunt that made the people around us turn their heads with displeasured expressions. Their looks, while short, did get under my skin but Darianna didn't even seem to have noticed.

"My math homework, help me out with it damn."

"Just gonna demand me like that, huh?"

"Yup."

I couldn't help but let out a laugh, "sure. I don't have anything to do after school anyways. But- nevermind."

The sweet smile left and a questioning expression appeared on her face instead. "What?"

"It's nothing. I forgot, by the way can you let go of my shoulders already?" I said with a stern voice but there was a clear smile that crept up on my lips. Darianna lifted her arms in defeat and scoffed.

"Sure, sure. No need to nag."

We laughed together as we walked up to the second floor together.

I'd nearly made a mistake.

I was gonna ask her why we couldn't study at her house but then realized that her home is a subject that shouldn't be mentioned. I didn't really know what was going on in that place but she'd always evade talking about it whenever I brought it up, so I just kinda realized to leave the subject alone.

But I would sometimes wonder what it was she was keeping hidden.

Chapter 3 - Bully And Bullied To Awkward Neighbours

F^emi

It was nearly 17.30 by the time I finally left school. Darianna wouldn't let me go until she understood everything and while I complained a lot it was pretty fun helping her and watching her suffer from not getting it. I chuckled at the memory of her contorted expressions while trying to understand the complex questions as I walked back home. Even though it was really late I didn't feel the need to worry about my parents and what they would say since they likely hadn't even noticed that I wasn't home. They were both doctors and sometimes it felt like they lived at the hospital with how long they'd disappear. I understood why so I didn't really hold it against them but it did make living at their large house feel scary for a young child.

My steps slowed and my gaze was stuck to the ground. A weak sigh left my body and I stopped gazing at the plain cement ground. I thought back to how Darianna had been pestering me about when I sat down next to

Ashton and how she'd beat him up for me. A laugh escaped my lips even though I had tried to keep it in, the fact I honestly couldn't tell who would win between them if they fought made it all funnier to me.

I got to my apartment door and put in the code and after went in. My steps on the stairs were the usual slow and heavy ones. 'Time for another game of will my parents be home today? Maybe I'll be hit with a suprise.' A small dry chuckle appeared after that thought.

I climed all the stairs and when I looked down to find my keys a strange black figure was at the corner of my eye, layed on the ground. 'A shoe?' My eyes traced the figure until it reached the top, it was a person, a familiar one.

Ashton Yang.

Freaking Ashton was laying by my doorstep, bloody and unconsious, well I thought he was. 'Should I get closer? Or maybe just leave him? Is he sleeping? Wait he has to be, but why here?!' Ashton being in this apartment wasn't shocking since he moved here and became my neighbour a few years ago, what was shocking was him being by my doorstep. I had made sure to never interact with him and we'd never met anyways except for some awkward moments where we'd throw out the trash or something. But never anything like this. My steps were light as my feet walked toward him, barely making a sound. I knelt down and inched closer to his face and it was clear that he was knocked out cold.

After having calmed down a bit I realized that he must've tried to get home after a fight but fainted once he reached my door. So the question was wether I'd just leave him or help him out with those injuries of his. My lips puckered to the side as I thought long and hard but I eventually grabbed him by the arms and lifted him up. Small mumbles and curses left my lips as I dragged him into my home. "You should really thank me for this, you're lucky I'm nice.."

I dragged him to the bathroom and placed him on the toilet. I brought out a cloth and drapped it in water and then turned to him. It was obvious he had several wounds, some under his clothes too most likely.

Did that mean I'd have to strip him? Only his shirt of course!

..No way, right..?

Chapter 4 - A Smile Towards Me

F emi

I had Ashton, my childhood bully sitting in my bathroom with his shirt lifted to take care of his wounds. Not once did I ever think that I'd reach a situation like this, I didn't know if I should've let out a chuckle or cry. The bruises covered his whole body, he was red and blue all over and I felt like I could cry just from looking at him. I didn't want to imagine what it would feel like to be him. The stench of alchohol covered the whole room, my nose started to sting from the smell and even though I wanted to cover my nose, cleaning him would be easier if I could use both of my hands. The red stained cloth went up and down his arm as I cleaned him and before I could pull away my hand to dip the cloth in water a hand grabbed my arm.

I gulped slowly and looked up.

Those gray eyes were locked to mine, it felt as though I couldn't escape his gaze. Even though I wanted to speak no words would come out. His eyes narrowed as he clearly inspected me, he looked around the room, he most likely tried to figure out what was going on. My arm stayed in his grasp and felt cold to his touch, from the water I had used to clean him.

He let out a sigh and let go of me. Moving away wasn't something I felt like doing even tho I could, I just looked down at the ground. My heart was beating so fast to the point it started to hurt. I smiled at my own stupidity for having put myself in a situation like this, taking Ashton to my house was obviously not gonna end in me having several heart attacks out of shock.

"Sorry."

My eyes widened at the words I had just heard, that deep voice just uttered a word I never thought I'd hear from him. "What?"

Was all I could say. My mind was empty and all I could think about was that "Sorry".

I got up and took a few steps back to give him some space. We were both looking at each other again and his eyebrows were furrowed, was he annoyed? I couldn't tell.

"Femi, sorry about how I used to treat you." He sighed.

He got up and walked right past me, not giving me a moment to process what he had just said. Sorry? To who? Me? He felt bad about what happened between us, to the point he'd apologize. That should be a good thing, right?

My face felt cold, my eyes darted around the bathroom with equipments spread around the floor. I took in a large breath and walked out the room, stomping my feet in the process. I grabbed Ashton a bit more forcefully than I'd intended to.

"I'm not done. There are more injuries I need to treat."

His eyes widened and then turned back to it's usual stern look. "Alright."

.

.

.

Ashton stood by my doorstep, his injuries all taken care of. I fidgeted with my fingers as I looked at him, the cold sweat ran down my neck and my throat felt dry.

"Thank you," I said in a quiet whisper.

He opened his mouth to say something but then closed it again, as if he was thinking of what to say.

"Why would you help me?"

His voice sent shivers down my spine, that voice of his was something that always scared me.

"I dunno. I just felt like it." I smiled. It was true, at the moment all I felt like doing was helping him, even though he had hurt me it was a long time ago.

A chuckle escaped his lips, "What a strange reason."

My heart stoped at the sight, at what I had just heard..

He turned around and left, leaving me alone in the chilly hallway.

'Is this the first time he's ever smiled towards me?'

Chapter 5 - I Want The Answer To Your Mystery

F emi

Ashton had always been many things to me, a question, one I'd never know the answer to. 'Does he hate me? Why'd he stop bothering me? Why'd be apologize?'

I'd always been too scared to get close, to hear what he had to say and understand but this time it felt different. Even though I could get hurt I didn't care, well I did care a bit but the urge to finally reach out and just ask him was stronger than my fear. Ashton being a mystery was something I feared but this time it made me drawn to him. I didn't like him, not at all, but I did want to know what was going through his mind. So I was gonna know, there was no need to hide and avoid him in fear anymore. Expecially after that apology.

.

.

.

After an average boring day, which became a bit more fun thanks to Darianna, I walked down my usual path home. Up ahead was Ashton, his raven hair was a bit russled from the wind, he was walking the same path as me obviously since we lived in the same apartment.

"Ashton!" I called out and immediatly regreted it after, while in my thoughts I was confident, once it actually came to talking to him I froze. I couldn't just walk up to him and go 'Hey Ashton I want to know more about you 'cus of how you've been acting these few years which has left me incredibly curious about you.' God no, I'd look like an idiot!

Ashton turned and looked at me with his usual cold expression and I felt the pressure under his gaze.

"Urm.. Well.. Your injuries! Are they better?"

His eyebrows furrowed in confusion, "yeah."

"Oh well that's good," I awkwardly laughed.

I took larger steps so that I could keep up to his walking and he later slowed his pace.

"Do you usually fight?" I asked.

"Why do you want to know?"

"Because I'm curious," I scoffed. "Isn't it obvious?"

He glanced at me with furrowed brows and then looked back forward, we continued walking in silence.

"Does your parents know about your fighting?" I looked up at him, "did they notice your injuries?"

"Why do you ask so many questions?" He grumbled and turned his face away from mine.

It seemed like I had gotten him a bit annoyed but even so I didn't feel scared, atleast not as scared as I'd usually would've. My palms were sweaty from nervousness and it felt like I had to muster all my strength just to speak but even so it got a bit easier. I wouldn't be able to learn anything if I only stayed and watched him from the side, so I had to speak.

"Because you're weird." I said with a chuckle.

"Don't push it crybaby."

I gasped loudly and turned to him in shock. "You did not just call me that! Don't say that ever again."

"And what're you gonna do about it?" He smirked.

"I'll-"

A sweet voice called out to Ashton which made me stop what I was saying. I hadn't noticed that we had already gotten to the entrance of the apartment, it went a bit faster than usual. The woman looked at me and Ashton with a warm smile, she looked somewhat similar to him. They both had tan skin and their noses were the same shape, thin and goes sligthly upright at the bottom.

"Femi is that you? You've grown so much!" she said with a friendly smile.

She laughed once she noticed my confused expression and spoke, "I'm Ashton's mother, I've seen you several times whenever I'd pick Ashton up from elementary school."

"Oh, urm.. It's nice meeting you." I gave her a small wave and tried to smile.

Ashton's mom stepped forward and grabbed my hands with gentleness. "Why don't you come over to our home? I've got several things I want to talk to you about."

'Wait what?'

Ashton didn't even stick around to listen and was already on his way to his home, while I stood, holding hands with his mom. Her eyes sparkled as if there was something she really wanted to tell me. I let out a sigh and nodded. 'Going into his home wasn't something I was expecting to happen now of all times..'

"Sure, I've got time to spare."

Chapter 6 - The Sweet Taste Of Blood

F^{emi}

We sat in the living room, only me and Ashton's mom. Ashton had left and gone to his room. She picked up a plate of cookies and handed them to me with a graceful smile. "Don't be shy, you can snack while we talk."

"Oh! You really don't- Well alright. Thank you." I couldn't say no to that face and caved in.

Mrs. Yang leaned back and turned to me, she was sitting next to me with a small distance between us. "How has it been going between you and Ashton?"

I nearly swallowed the cookies wrong because of her question. "Well it's been.. alright. We don't really talk much but I do want to get closer to him."

"That's nice to hear, glad to know that my son is gonna make more friends." She laughed and then held my hand. Her touch was soft and warm, just what I had imagined the hands of a mother to be.

"I know that my son didn't treat you well back then, I'm so sorry for his actions."

"No, it's alright, really!" I said with a shaky, flustered voice. She only eyed me with a sorrowful expression and nodded.

"You're too kind." She smiled again but this one wasn't as gleeful as the last ones.

"Back then I thought that you two were good friends and that it was only friendly teasing. I was too caught up in my own problems to notice that my son was hurting and in turn ended up hurting others."

I couldn't say anything back and only stared at her tearfilled eyes.

"If I had been a better mother then you wouldn't have gone through that. I'm sorry."

I opened my mouth to say something back but the words just couldn't come out, was there even something for me to say? I simply nodded and uttered a quiet "Thank you".

After having talked for a while I got up to leave but before I could Mrs. Yang stopped me. "It was nice finally getting to talk to you."

A small grin appeared on my lips, "likewise."

"Femi, if my son ever gets into any trouble please tell me."

"I will."

.

.

.

I laid sunken in my bed and thought back to what had happened today. Mrs. Yang was a lot sweeter than I'd thought she'd be and even though she really resembled her son their personalities couldn't be any further apart. I couldn't help but chuckle at the thought and hugged my pillow tightly. The slight breeze that came from the open window was a bit too chilly so I got up to close it and when I looked down I noticed something. Ashton was outside and was headed somewhere, it was the middle of the night and it didn't seem like he was going out to buy groceries.

'Is he gonna get into another fight?'

I bit my lower lip and then left to get my jacket and went out. I could barely see where I was going and the complete silence outside made my heart drop. It felt like someone could jump out and attack me at any second. I followed Ashton from a distance, just to make sure he wasn't gonna do anything stupid, alright? Don't judge me. I soon stopped at a empty, rundown house which Ashton entered. I peeked through the open door and could hear voices, mainly screaming and shouting. This definitely didn't look like a normal meeting between friends.

The clouds moved and made the moon more visible, thanks to that there was a bit more light. From what I could see inside, the guys were in a very heated argument but Ashton still kept his distance until the guy snapped and ran towards Ashton to punch him. Before I knew it I was infront of Ashton and took the punch for him.

The taste of blood was the only thing I could think about.

It was oddly sweet.

Chapter 7 - Silent Nights Filled With Tears

F^{emi}

I staggered backwards but was held upright by firm hands, Ashtons hands, and when I looked up too see his face he was making a expression I had only ever seen him do once before. It was when one of his friends had made a joke and went too far with it, it was something about his mother. That guy didn't come back to school for a solid month after Ashton was done with him. His eyes were dark and cold. I could tell just from looking at him that he wanted to beat up the guy that had just hit me but I couldn't let that happen. I came here to stop him from fighting, not be the reason for it!

I tugged at his arm and pulled him out of there, it took all my strength just to move him. The guys were running after us and shouting but we soon escaped and hid in a dark alleyway. I could hear distant shouting and footsteps but it didn't sound like it was getting any closer so I leaned back to the wall and sighed in relief. Ashton was looking at me with his usual frown, there was something he wanted to say, most likely to scold me. But I wasn't gonna let him so I spoke before he got a chance to.

"You shouldn't get into fights so often," my voice came out as a whisper,

Ashton remained silent. My gaze wandered to the starry night sky, covered in colours that gave me a sense of relief. "Your mom," I sighed, "if you continue like this she'll worry."

I chuckled at my own words, to have parents that worry for you or are even present enough to notice your wounds.. what would that be like?

Cold hands rubbing against my cheek broke me out of my thoughts. My eyes weren't on the sky anymore but instead at the man in front of me. "To lecture me, while in this condition.. Do you realize how stupid you look?"

His eyes were glued to mine, stuck in a gaze I couldn't dare look away from. There was a softness to his touch, as if he was holding glass as fragile as a feather.

I finally realized just how much blood was spilling from my nose and covered it up instantly. My white shirt was now died red and I sighed at the mess. I'd have to wash it as soon as I got home, my favourite shirt just had to be stained in blood of all things..

My body started shaking and I could feel how my knees went weak, small teardrops fell from my eyes and I didn't even bother to wipe them. Pretty delayed reaction, I know. A girl like me wasn't exactly used to situations like this. Dealing with a group of scary men, out at midnight, getting punched and messing up my shirt. I couldn't deal with all these emotions stirring up inside me so I did what I do best, cry.

And the crying only made me feel worse, which led me to cry even more, it was a vicious cycle.

To cry in front of Ashton, the person who made me grow to hate this side of me the most wasn't something I'd thought I'd do in a million years.

It was a silent cry, the only thing that could be heard was the teardrops hitting the ground but it didn't stop me from feeling any less weak.

My eyes stayed locked to the ground, I couldn't look up, I didn't want to look up.

Ashton had most likely noticed my crying yet he still didn't say anything. He only remained silent. Did he not know what to say? Or did he simply just not want to say anything? Either way I didn't have a problem with it.

"Do you still consider me a crybaby?"

The question sat at the air which made me feel stupid for opening my mouth and saying something like that. I looked up, just so I could see his face. If I could read his expression maybe I'd feel less awkward?

But the expression I saw wasn't one I had expected.

His lips were curved in a smirk.

"What a stupid question," he said. "You'll always be my crybaby."

Chapter 8 - If Looks Could Kill

F emi

"-emi. Femi!"

"Huh? What?"

Darianna gave me an annoyed look and went back to speaking. "Where's your mind at? Have you even been listening to anything I've been saying?"

"Nope. Sorry, just got a lot stuck on my mind."

"Damn, like what?"

I gave her a playful grin and wrapped my arm around hers. "None of your business." I chuckled. She scoffed in a exaggerated tone and then smiled my way.

"If you wanna be that way then okay. Don't start complaining to me though if I start repeating my words whenever it looks like your mind is in the gutter."

Her words made my smile grow wider, "yeah, yeah. Don't worry I won't."

My mind had been all over the place after what had happened yesterday. The words he told me couldn't leave, they stayed etched into my brain.

"You'll always be my crybaby."

'My', as in his, his crybaby? What?

No matter how I tried to make sense of it I just couldn't. Whenever it felt like I had come to understand him even a bit more he'd pull something that'd show that I still didn't know him at all.

The smirk he gave me, was it supposed to mean something?

It all just felt like a strange dream, something that just couldn't have happened. But the stinging on my nose would bring me back to reality and confirm that it all wasn't just some strange dream.

'I wonder, what could possibly be going through Ashton's mind right now?'

We soon enough got to class and took our usual seats. This time my seat hadn't been stolen by some rando, so sitting next to Ashton again wasn't necessary. Well being his seatmate could've been a good way to get closer and understand him more. But after what happened yesterday I needed a moment for myself to calm down.

The teacher entered the room and threw her stacks of papers on her table. She looked at us with a wide grin. "Alright class! Today we'll be working on a fun group project. You'll be in groups of four. It'll be about what we went through last week: social media and how it's affecting the youth."

The class remained silent and the teacher grunted at our reaction. "You get to pick your partners."

Immediately the class erupted into cheers and everyone moved over and rearranged their seats to be with their friends. I stayed seated but exchanged glances with Darianna, we were both smiling to each other and soon enough she got up, carrying her backpack with her. Her smile faded and she stopped walking, I followed where her eyes were looking to see what caused such a reaction from her. To my right stood Ashton, his eyes cold.

"Join my group."

The way he said it made it clear I didn't really have an option to decline. He didn't even bother to phrase it as a question.

I nodded slowly and then glanced to the corner of my eye to see Darianna's reaction, which was very not pleased. She looked like she was about to pop a blood vessel. I gave her a sheepish grin hoping that would calm her down a bit and it did. Well she was still very pissed, but her expression had turned to a deadly scowl instead. Ashton had taken a seat next to me and Darianna moved one of the chairs to sit in front of me.

Her eyes stayed locked on Ashton as if he were her prey while Ashton kept his eyes to his phone.

"Who will be our fourth member?" I asked.

"Mako, he's not here right now but he should pull up to class in about ten minutes."

Darianna clicked her tounge but I ignored it and nodded. "Alright."

Was this a weird prank of his? Was he trying to torture me or maybe this was a strange new way of bullying? Just when I felt like taking some time to gather my thoughts he does this.

'Ashton Yang really is a person I'll never understand.'

Chapter 9 - Messy Breakups Can't Be Avoided

D arianna

My eyes were focused on Ashton and Femi kept on giving me small worried glances but I didn't care. He hadn't seemed to notice me, or maybe I wasn't important enough for him to notice me but even so I made sure to keep my eyes on him. 'I don't know what he's playing at but I'm not gonna let him do anything to her.'

Femi had told me some stories about their childhood and even if she'd smile my way and tell me that she was over it, it was clear that she wasn't. The way her chocolate brown eyes would shimmer whenever she'd bring up their past, turning red by the corners, struggling to hold in her tears.

It pissed me off.

It all pissed me off.

And it was his fault.

The bags that were thrown on the table broke me out of my thoughts and I looked to see who had just done that. Dark eyes glimmered as they looked into mine with a wide smile. The guy took a seat next to mine and slumped down, bumping his knee to the table on the process.

"So what did I miss?" he asked, his smile still in wide display.

"The thing from last week, we have to write a essay about it," I said.

"We should plan out how we'll divide this project," Femi added in a low voice, it looked like Mako hadn't even heard what she said for a second there.

Ashton put down his phone and sighed. His body shifted to Mako and Mako looked back at him in return.

"We have to get this done by next week," Ashton said.

My jaw tightened just from hearing his voice and for just a moment his eyes caught mine. We both looked away immediately like we meant nothing to each other, which we basically did.

"Alright then." Mako slumped further into his seat and looked up. "If we're gonna be stuck with each other for around a week then why not get a littler closer?"

"What?" my voice came out in a more threatening manner than it was supposed to.

"How about going to a party? I was invited recently to Jessica's party and had no one to go with." Mako pointed towards Ashton. "Since this jerk over here didn't even bother to think about going with me."

He let out an exaggerated sigh and then went back to his rambling. "If we're gonna be stuck together doing a trashy essay then we might as well make it more fun by growing closer with each other."

We all stayed silent. Femi looked like she was honestly contemplating it but was leaning more towards the option of not going while Ashton looked bored out of his mind. As for me, the choice was still unclear.

"When does the party start?" I asked.

Mako gave me a smirk, "around ten-fifty."

At a time like that I'd be out of home.

I could come up with a solid excuse. Would I even need one when it came to him? Either way between staying there and being out partying the choice was clear as day.

"I'm in."

Femi looked up at me with wide eyes and them stumbled with her words. "I'll go too!"

We all turned to look at Ashton waiting for his answer but he remained silent.

Mako let out a sigh, "I'll text you the address and the time so you don't forget."

Ashton picked up his phone without saying anything and we all started working on the project silently.

.

.

.

Femi and I parted ways at our usual place and for the rest of the time I walked home alone in silence. I stopped by a convenience store to go buy a drink. I wasn't even thirsty but anything that'd stall me from getting home was fine by me. Before I could leave a loud smack echoed through the thin walls. Soon after a woman bumped into me and ran out with tears in her eyes. It was just a short glimpse that I caught of her but I could tell that her mascara was a mess.

I peeked behind me too see who could've caused such a scene only to see familiar dark brown eyes.

His sunkissed skin had a weird yellow tint to it thanks to the dingy lighting.

Mako. He stood there with a red cheek and I jumped to the nearest isle to hide.

'Did Mako just have a messy break up in a convenience store?'

'And did I seriously just witness that?'

Chapter 10 - Silent Nights Filled With Laughs

D arianna

We stood outside the store, a small wet chill reaching my finger tips from my drink. The small breeze made the stench of cigarettes drift past me. The occasional clinks of the convenience store door opening or closing added to my annoyance.

"So is she your girlfriend?"

"No."

"Oh."

I took small sips from my drink and didn't move from my spot. It was a weird silence, there wasn't really much to say but I didn't feel awkward over it.

"You're not gonna ask about who she is to me?"

I glanced upwards to see Mako looking at me with a solemn expression. It was one that I'd never seen him have before. He was usually just smiling and laughing, goofing off with that jerk.

"It doesn't really have anything to do with me."

"Sounds more like you just don't care."

"Maybe I don't."

A smile crept up on his lips after what I said and I couldn't help but stare. His smiles were some of the brightest I'd ever seen. I'd sometimes wonder about what he had that'd have him smiling like that— whatever it was, I wanted it too.

"She isn't my girlfriend." He looked up at the night sky. "Just some girl that got a bit too attached to me after we met at a party."

He placed his hand on his cheek and started rubbing it. "Ouch, that really stings."

In a daze my hand moved to his injury.

"Ahh, yeah. That shit looks real nasty, should probably put some ice on that." I said with a awkward chuckle.

My hand traced his cheek and felt the smoothness of it. His skin was awfully warm, like he had just been working out.

His chin was chiseled, his lips a soft colour, his eyebrows were full and his eyes,

they were black with the slightest bits of gray in them.

Those eyes, I wanted to stare at them for as long as I could.

They glimmered under the night sky and stared back at mine. I backed away from him. My chest felt tight and I looked away to the other side of the dark road, with metal fences surrounding it. My eyes stayed locked on looking at the surroundings, I didn't turn to look back at him again. It felt weird, my body felt weird, like I could hear my own heartbeat thudding in my ears.

"Shouldn't you get home?" he asked.

I should've.

I couldn't stay out too long all the time.

"No."

"Me neither."

We stood in silence with only the sounds of the surroundings to be heard. The distant laughter, ruffling leaves, and our quiet breaths were the only things my ears focused on.

It was a comforting feeling, one that made my body feel lighter.

'Strange.'

Chapter 11 - Just Stay A Little Longer

Femi

Some days had passed since we had started the group project and Mako had mentioned the party, well today was that day. I had gone on a shopping spree with Darianna, one she forced me into, so that I'd have some clothes that'd actually fit the occasion. It was shocking that she'd actually accepted Mako's offer about the party, she had always been a party girl but for her to be fine with Mako, Ashton's friend, was what threw me off.

Asking about it would be trivial, she'd most likely would've avoided the question or given me a half hearted reply so I just chose to not even bother.

I met up with Darianna, her hair was in a slicked back puff as per usual. We then headed for the party and saw Mako inside. He was letting loose, a drink in one hand while holding a woman in the other. He was showing off his charming smile again and laughing with everyone around him. He soon after noticed us and let go of the woman to walk up to us. "So how do you like it?" he smiled.

"I've been at better parties," Darianna said and took a gulp of her drink. Mako chuckled at her words.

"Really? Better invite me to them when you get the chance."

"I'll think about it," she smirked.

Mako turned to look at me, "how about you?"

"Me? Oh, well.. it's alright." Honestly the music was a bit too loud for my liking but I was better off keeping that for myself.

The music was making my ears ring and the place felt like it was getting hotter by the minute. I felt thankful over choosing to wear a sleeveless dress. My eyes wandered the place as if it was searching for something, searching for someone.

"Looking for Ashton?" Mako said with a warm smile.

"N- no, well.."

"I think I saw him going to the second floor, you should find him there." He pointed up and I nodded. I turned to leave but felt a hand grasp my arm.

"Don't run off alone," Darianna said. Her light brown eyes were filled with a sense of worry. So I smiled at her.

"Right, but wouldn't it be better to stay with Mako? So he doesn't end up alone. Plus you two seem to be getting along well. " She frowned at me and then clicked her tongue.

"He can keep himself company," she walked in front of me, still holding my hand and dragged me out of the crowd. "Now come on, let's go."

We squeezed through the people chilling on the stairs and got to the second floor. "Why would Ashton come to a party? That's not very like him," I muttered.

"Why not go ask him yourself? You seem to have taken a interest in him. Are you maybe into bullies or something?" She smirked with furrowed brows, clearly taunting me.

"It's not like that!"

"Hmmm, sure," she hummed. "I still don't trust that guy though."

"He's not that bad.. anymore."

"I'll have to see that for myself," she mumbled.

My eyes instantly caught the tall boy standing at the edge of hallway, his gray eyes were visible even from all the way over here. The tiny eyebrow piercing shimmered under the light. Before I knew it I was standing right in front of him with Darianna by my side. I breathed in slowly to calm my heart. 'Why is my heart beating so fast?'

"Why'd you come to the party?" I asked.

"Doesn't really have anything to do with you, does it?"

"Ahh.. really? Or did you perhaps come since you knew I'd be here?" His eyes sharpened and then went back to his stoic expression.

"Believe whatever you want, crybaby." He smirked.

His smirk grew wider as he noticed how my body jolted over his words. He glanced over at me and Darianna and then stepped between us.

"Seems like I have no reason to stay so I might as well leave."

My hand reached out to touch him but stopped halfway. I wanted to tell him to wait but couldn't. Why did I even want him to stay? Was it just because I was intrigued by him like I've been thinking all this time, or was it something more? Just..

"Why.."

Chapter 12 - A Door To The Face

T w: sexual assault/harassment

Femi

Darianna and Mako were having their usual banter and while I would join in here and there, maybe even chuckle sometimes it still didn't feel like I was really there with them. My mind was stuck in another place. 'Did he really leave? Maybe he went back?'

I took a step back and went back up to the second floor. The place was filled with a mixture of smells that did not fit each other at all, alcohol, sweat and smoke. It was bad, I scrunched my nose in disgust and covered it with my hands.

I felt a presence behind me and turned around only to be disappointed to see who it wasn't.

"Hey there beautiful," he smiled. He put one hand on my shoulder and smirked.

"Uhm, I.. I don't think I know you. Do you need anything?"

He bit his lower lip and I felt a chill run down my spine. There was something about that gaze that felt unnatural. "Actually I think my friend is waiting for me. I've got to go." I walked past him but was pulled back to his sweaty chest. I let out a deep sigh and hoped that I wouldn't just randomly start crying.

"What I need is you baby."

"I'd rather you don't call me that," my voice came out in a softer manner than it was supposed to.

He spun me around so that our faces were now facing each other and started tracing down my body. His touch felt slimy and cold. I wanted to push him away but my body didn't move, like it wasn't my own. He pressed his chapped lips on my neck and started kissing it. He left wet kisses all over my neck.

"Can you- can you please stop?"

He looked at me with cold eyes and a wide grin. His smile looked so different from Mako's, his was devilish and cruel, one I didn't want to look at.

"Are you crying?" he asked with a smirk. "So cute."

Anger erupted in me, he had just violated me but had the gull to call me cute because of my crying? Could he be any worse? I kicked him in the knee and ran out, nearly twisting my ankles in the process because of my heels. I could hear how he was grunting behind me and saying several curses but I didn't look back.

I got out and breathed in the fresh air, taking big breaths, gasping for the air. The small breeze tickled my skin that was drenched in sweat.

"Femi?" A familiar cold voice, one that'd always have my hairs stand on end, called out to me but I didn't turn around.

His steps got closer and closer, soon enough he was standing right behind me. I couldn't hold in my hiccups and sniffing. He'd already caught on, anyone would've.

"Turn around."

I stood still.

"I said turn around," his voice was sterner this time.

The taste of blood tickled my tongue from how hard I was biting my lower lip.

He grabbed me by the elbow and spun me to face him. His cold eyes went soft once he saw my bloodshot eyes. "What happened?"

I wiped my tears and gave him a smile but I could tell how wonky and fake it looked.

"I've always been a crybaby so it really isn't that big of a deal. I just walked into a door, that's all." I laughed but my voice cracked in the middle of it.

I pushed his arm off me, "I'm gonna go home now, I'm pretty exhausted."

"I'll go with you."

"I'd rather go alone, thanks."

"No."

I bit my lower lip and glared up at him.

"I want to be alone!" I shouted.

A weak sigh escaped my lips as I took a step back.

"Sorry. Just leave me alone, that's all I want."

Chapter 13 - A Simple Overreaction Yet Again

F emi

The walk home was unusually silent, my mind was blank, maybe there just wasn't much to think about. It was just a kiss on the neck— no big deal— overreacting again— that's all. I ran straight to the bathroom once I got home, not even bothering to check if my parents were here.

My black box braids dropped over my face, I had to push them behind my ears to see clearly. The view from the mirror was an expected sight, my eyes bloodshot, lower lip swollen and my dark skin dripping with sweat. My eyes widened at the sight of my neck, the whole thing covered in hickeys. I'd thought he'd only left one or two, at most. But this, this was way beyond that. My lower lip quivered and I held back from biting it again.

I got undressed and entered the bath. I'd wash it all away, the cold touch of his— his slimy kisses— all of it would disappear after today. The more I remembered, the harsher the scrubbing got. My anger, sadness, disappointment, disgust, I poured it all into scrubbing my body clean. Even if my skin ripped I wouldn't stop. My emotions had to be let out somehow. I couldn't just cry. Could I?

That's weak.

I'm weak.

I stood there doing nothing.

I practically let him touch me.

Did I have a right to complain?

What was crying gonna do?

.

.

School went as normal as it usually did, or as normal as it could. Darianna hadn't called me yesterday about how I randomly ran off or asked me anything. It was as if she didn't know.

"If you're gonna leave then tell me next time so I don't have to have Mr. Grumpy talk to me," Darianna grumbled while pinching the straw in her juice.

"What?"

She looked at me with a stoic expression. "The party, Ashton told me and Mako that you got a bad stomachache and went home. I get that you were feeling sick but couldn't you tell me yourself?" she asked and then gave me a smirk. "Or was it that bad?"

"Oh. C'mon don't say stuff like that," I giggled but did it sound too forced?

She pointed to my neck, "by the way, what's up with all those bandages?"

"Mosquito bites."

My reply came out a lot faster and sharper than I intended. Darianna looked at me with a cold glance and then smiled.

"Really? Aight then."

Ashton was nowhere to be seen the whole day. I had planned to avoid him after what happened at the party but it seemed like it wasn't needed. Until I felt the air in the hallway shift in a way it only did when one person would walk through it, Ashton. His eyes were locked on one target, me, and I could see from the corner of my eye how Darianna was watching me while sipping her juice. Before I could react Ashton grabbed my arm and pulled me out of the busy hallway. I looked at Darianna with pleading eyes but she only brought out her phone and walked off. She waved me a goodbye and said good luck.

Darianna wasn't the type to just abandon me like that, especially with Ashton. Had she noticed that something was off with me? But I didn't have time to think about that as Ashton pulled me into a dark corner with only us there.

"What?" I managed to say without a stutter which honestly shocked me.

"What happened yesterday?" His voice was cold enough to send me chills.

"Please let go of my hand." Was all I could whisper. He let go but still kept his eyes on me.

His eyes darkened as soon as he noticed my bandages. "Your neck."

I gulped slowly and then rubbed my neck as I looked down. "Just some mosquito bites, that's all."

I was ready to go but before I could he grabbed one of the bandages on my neck and pulled it off. I could feel myself going dizzy and didn't want to stay long enough to hear what he had to say and ran of.

It was embarrassing.

Of all people, why'd he have to know?

And why like this..?

.

.

.

A/N

Just to make things clear I do not agree with Femi's thoughts.

She made her objection clear but the guy wouldn't listen. Even if the objection was unclear for him she still didn't give him a definite 'yes' therefore he shouldn't have touched her like that.

She's the victim while he's the aggressor.

She did nothing wrong but ofc Femi can't see that since she's not in the right headspace rn.

Chapter 14 - A broken Nose Is The Best Revenge

Femi

The food in the cafeteria tasted duller than usual. Darianna had been talking to me casually but it felt like I couldn't give her natural replies. Had I forgotten how to speak?

There was nothing much that was crossing my mind, like it had come to a halt. I looked up from my food to see a man pass by me with a smirk. He gave me a wink and sat down. Even though that party had been very dark I could still recognize him. That blonde hair and blue eyes, he was the one from then. My body went cold and all the food that I had eaten was fighting to come out. Darianna passed me a drink and then looked back at the guy. "Do you know John?"

"W- who..? Oh, him," I stuttered. "No, I just, I don't know. Think I saw him at the party before. He was probably there when I walked into a door. It was so embarrassing!" I took a sip of the drink she gave me which calmed my nerves a bit.

"Damn so you walked into a door and had stomach problems? Your luck is in a different league girl," Darianna smiled and I smiled back.

I glanced back to see John, who was now sitting with his friends, still smirking at me. His cold blue eyes didn't look away from me even if I glanced away. I could still feel his gaze. My leg kept on tapping in an uneven tempo under the table and stopped once he spoke.

"Yup, I made out with a hot chick at the party yesterday," he smirked. "She was totally into me."

"No way dude! You always get all the girls," his friend laughed.

"Does she go to this school? I wanna know which girl you got this time." Another friend joined in.

John licked his lips as he looked at me. "Well.."

Before I could react, before I could say no or even do anything John was already on the floor, his nose bloody. Ashton stood there with blood on his knuckles and wiped them away like he was just getting rid of dust. John tried to get back up to hit him but Ashton stepped on his hand which made John fall down in defeat. Ashton bent down and grabbed John by the collar to whisper something in his ear and then let him go which made John hit the floor with a loud thud.

He soon got up and left the cafeteria while John struggled to get up with his friends by his side helping him. Soon after a teacher followed out of the cafeteria with a bright red face.

Darianna got cut off by me springing up from my seat to run after Ashton.

The emotions in me were running wild.

A sense of relief and happiness but also anger. He couldn't just punch someone like that, why did he even do that? My heart tightened in my chest and it felt like I was close to tears. Whenever I was feeling overly emotional my tears would come, even if I didn't want them to.

I stopped once I heard the familiar teachers voice berating Ashton and telling him to go to his office before school closed. Ashton only said a quiet okay and that voice of his nearly made my heart skip a beat.

The teacher soon after left and I walked over to Ashton. He looked at me with a stoic expression, it was kind of funny. You never would've guessed that he broke someone's nose just a second ago from how casual his expression was.

"What do you want?" His deep voice echoed throughout my ears. I forgot what I was supposed to say for a second but snapped out of it.

"Why did you do that?" His expression made it clear that he was gonna ask, do what? So I spoke before he could. "You know what, why'd you punch that guy?"

"His yapping was getting annoying so I shut him up, that's all."

I bit my lower lip and looked down. "Is it because of what he did?"

He let out a sigh, "I don't know what you're talking about."

He walked past me with his shoulders slumped and his hair so messy you'd think he just got out of bed.

I looked at him from afar, longer than I needed, and muttered a quiet thank you.

Chapter 15 - Looking At The Ember Sky

A^{shton}

That guy couldn't keep his mouth shut could he? Just kept on talking and talking, someone had to shut him up. And the way she looked, those chocolate brown eyes of hers looked like they were gonna cry at any second. They were wide with fear and her skin was going pale, that was exactly how she used to look at me until recently. What even caused the change for her? Not like it really mattered.

"Ashton!"

I looked up at the teacher that had been berating me for a hour now. He'd been pretty happy with me for how I hadn't been in as many fights anymore. Which wasn't really true, I just wasn't fighting in school as much anymore. Either way the guy kept on going about how he expected better from me and how I needed to be suitably punished which I didn't really care for.

Oh shit.

'My mom's gonna hear about this.'

I'd heard bits and pieces of what she told Femi when she came over to my house. The walls were always too thin for their own good.

If she heard about me getting suspended for breaking some jackass' nose she'd probably go crazy. Well there wasn't much to be done now.

I got up from my seat since I didn't need to hear more of his rambling and left the school. The sky had already turned to a cmber colour which meant that my mom was probably home by now. I looked down only to see someone else staring at the sky. Her dark braids that reached her back flowing in the wind and her dark brown skin had a orange glow to it thanks to the sun that made her look more alive than ever.

She turned around and looked at me with a gaze that made it seem like she was lost in thought and then bit her lower lip. It was a weird habit of hers that I couldn't look away from. She walked up to me with furrowed brows.

"How'd it go?" she tried to look stern but I could see how she was clenching her backpacks strap from from being nervous.

"Got suspended for a week, nothing big." Her eyes widened in shock and her grip got even firmer on the strap.

"Nothing big?! How will your mom feel about this? Oh.. this is all my fault."

I was gonna say something back but noticed those damn bandages on her neck again and felt how my jaw tightened. Before I could reply Femi ran past me.

"If I explain the situation to the teacher then maybe he'll understand and give you a lighter punishment," she shouted, still holding the backpack strap but looser this time. Her eyes looked into mine with an determination I'd never seen her have before and soon after she ran into the school.

This was so stupid.

It really wasn't that big of a deal.

That carefree nature of hers always ticked me off.

I turned to walk home but my legs couldn't move. I stood firmly in my spot, waiting for her, waiting for her to come back with that stupid smile of hers saying she did it.

It wasn't really like I cared about that suspension but even so I didn't want to move.

The crybaby Femi who'd never been able to look me in the eye was now acting like this, facing me with determination, doing something for my sake.

Sometimes I'd wonder, what was going through that mind of hers?

Chapter 16 - It Wasn't Your Fault

Femi

I went back out still feeling how my heart was thumping from the conversation with the teacher. He'd been a lot kinder that I'd though he'd be and gave me soft smile when I explained the situation.

I saw Aston leaning against a metal fence as he scrolled through his phone. As soon as the door slammed shut Ashton turned his head to me. "So how'd it go?"

I smiled at his words and felt so airy, like all my problems had been lifted off my shoulders. I couldn't hold in my laughter, "He's gonna get expelled! They'll actually expel John for what happened." I rubbed my eyes and my smile faded.

"You'll still be suspended for three days though, I wasn't able to do much, sorry."

Ashton didn't reply back and walked forward and I soon caught up to him to walk by his side. "I probably wouldn't have been able to do anything if it weren't for you," I muttered.

Ashton stayed silent for a moment and then spoke, "I didn't do anything. It was all you."

My body felt warm from his words but maybe it was just from the sun. "I think I'll tell Darianna about what happened." My voice barely came out in a whisper.

"Why?"

I sighed and looked up at the beautiful sky that reminded me of romantic sunsets.

"I want to tell her, because she's my best friend."

He glanced my way and then went back to looking forward.

"Honestly I don't think it'll be easy, but you know and even my teacher does, but the one I really want to tell myself is Darianna." I turned to look at him even though he wasn't looking at me.

"Just getting it out would maybe," my voice started to tremble, "maybe it'll help me move on."

I let out a large sigh and smiled.

"I've gone a bit off course but I'll go back to my original goal."

Ashton looked at me with furrowed brows which made me chuckle. It was so clear that he was confused and that was honestly kind of cute.

Wait what?

.

.

I sat on a bench in the deserted park as Darianna was swinging her legs back and forth. She was waiting for me to speak. She wasn't pressuring me to say something and only sat in silence, basically telling me to take my time, that she'd wait however long I needed her to. The grass was dry and made a rustling sound whenever her feet would brush past it while swinging. The sky was a deep blue colour, one that looked cold and lonesome.

"Hey."

Darianna's feet stopped swinging but she didn't look at me.

"You're probably aware that something happened right?" I chuckled.

She gave me a smile, "yeah."

I nodded and looked back at the sky filled with stars and a moon that shone so brightly.

"Well at that party.. a guy, well he gave me a few hickeys– even when I told him to stop. So y'know, well yeah, I got a bit sad over it.. Just me overacting aga–" My words got cut off once I saw the way she was looking at me. Her eyes were wide open and her brows furrowed. I could see the fuming anger in her eyes but also the deep sadness.

"You don't need to.. ah.. Well.." The words wouldn't come out, that stinging feeling was coming back.

Darianna wrapped me in a tight hug, all the air nearly left my body.

"I'm sorry that I couldn't protect you," she whispered.

"Protect me? It's not like you're my mom.. hah," I laughed but I could hear how my voice cracked.

"I'm so sorry Femi. It wasn't your fault."

And with that I started bawling, I couldn't hold it in anymore. All those pent up emotions were released through my tears. I gripped her shirt and cried into her, not letting go. My mind went dizzy but I could hear her whisper sorry over and over again. The soft embrace, quiet whispers and muffled cries made my heart finally feel a little lighter.

Chapter 17 - Comparisons Are Never Fun

D arianna

The room was dim and cold with clothes splattered all over the floor. I had to drag my feet to even get to my bed. I sat down and brought out my computer so that I could work on my essay but all I could do was stare at the empty white page. No words could enter my mind, the things that happened to Femi were still rummaging through my mind. My hand twitched and I felt the sudden urge to beat up John again but it Ashton already beat me to it. 'He didn't do so badly there, I'll give him that.'

I shut my computer and laid down on my bed and was hit by the smell of cheese puffs, I really needed to get these sheets washed. My eyelids felt heavy and could barely stay open. I was ready to sleep even without having changed to my pj's and since I'd already taken a shower right after I got home from school I didn't have to think about that.

I let out a groan and shut my eyes, ready to feel at peace when I heard heavy footsteps that made me spring up. My body was up but I still kept my eyes to the dirty floor. I could feel his presence by the door but he wasn't saying anything and I wasn't gonna be the first one to speak. I mentally strangled myself over having forgotten to shut my door.

"Look at you Darianna, you look like a pig living in a pen," he snickered. "It's filthy, clean your room better."

'If I wasn't so busy cleaning the whole house after you while studying day and night to get good grades so you won't kill me then sure, maybe I'd have more time to clean my room.' Is what I wanted to say but instead all I could do was clench my jaw.

"What woman can't even do that?"

I let out a groan at his stupid words which ticked my father off more, I should've been more quiet.

"You remind me of your mother, beautiful but stupid." His voids were sharp and kept me on edge. "Barely even knew how to take care of herself, that's why she ended up like that," he sighed.

'Okay, I get it.'

I couldn't even mutter those words, if there was even a slightest chance of him hearing them he would've gotten even angrier.

"Your mother." He paused. "She was nothing more than a whore."

I looked at him with wide eyes and saw how dark his eyes were as they looked at me, so judgeful and cold.

"Don-"

"Quiet Darianna!" he shouted.

"If you don't get your act together you'll end up just like her, running off with some man, abandoning your own family," he said through gritted teeth.

"One day I'll move out of this shitty household." I glared.

He crossed his arms over his chest, "on your own? You'll need a man by your side just like your mother did. Will you use your body to survive?"

Those words filled me with anger, my body started to heat up and my breathing became rugged. I stood up and took a step forward with my jaw clenched and furrowed brows, I knew I must've looked stupid to him.

"Shut the fuck up." I breathed out, my voice was low and dark. His eyebrow twitched up and his glare became sharper.

"What did you say?"

Silence filled the room and the room had become even colder, to the point where I could feel myself start trembling.

"I said, shut the fuck up."

His eyes went wide and he lifted his hand, "don't you dare speak to your father that way!"

I ducked past him and ran out of the room, my heart kept on beating faster and faster, to the point where it felt like it would jump out of my chest. I ran out of the house and into the dimly lit street and gasped for air, like it was the first time I'd ever breathed in my life.

The tears couldn't stop coming and I didn't even want to bother to wipe them away, I just stood, at some random part of the street alone.

I took out my phone and called Femi but she didn't pick up. Couldn't really blame her since it was twelve-thirty right now and she was always the type to fall asleep early.

So I rummaged through my contacts to see if there was anyone I could call and landed on one. I stared at his number as my finger hovered over the call button.

I needed someone, anyone.

'Just pick up, please.'

I pressed the button and felt how my throat went dry as I heard his calm breathing.

"Hey?"

Chapter 18 – All You Need Is Someone

Darianna

My lower lip quivered once I heard his voice, which was even deeper than usual, through the phone.

"Hey?"

No words could come out and I could only cry silently as he sat through the other line confused.

"Wait are you crying?" His voice was filled with a strange sense of urgency.

"Mhmm."

"Is there.. Is there a reason you called me?" His voice was low and soothing.

I stayed silent for a moment and sniffed.

"I wanted to hear your voice," I sighed.

He didn't say anything back and I had nothing more to say. The wind got a bit more aggressive which made my hands burn with frost. "Hold on, are you outside?" he asked.

"Yeah." My voice came out as a whisper. "I don't want to stay home."

I soon regretted having said that as Mako went silent again. There were sounds of someone zipping something up and clothes moving around.

"What are you doing?" I asked.

"I'm going out. Where are you so we can meet?"

My heart clenched and my eyes darted around the empty streets. "We can meet at the convenience store instead."

"Alright," he said and even though I couldn't see his face I could still tell that he was smiling.

.

.

We stood outside the convenience store, the same spot as last time, as I held a icy lemon soda that irritated my skin.

Mako would glance at me sometimes and say stupid jokes but other than that he never really asked anything that could be related to what caused me to turn out like this. I appreciated the gesture, what I needed wasn't to talk to someone about it, I just needed someone by my side. That's all.

Mako took my cheek in his hand and rubbed under my eye in gently. "Your tears have dried."

"Yeah."

"I don't think I'll be crying again for a while though." I smiled. "Today was just a little worse than usual."

Which was true, I was used to my fathers annoying berating's but today I already had a lot stuck on my mind 'cause of Femi and then the words about my mother made me snap. A weak sigh escaped my lips as I remembered what had happened again. The corner of my eyes started to fill with tears again.

Mako was looking at me with such warmth I nearly lost my breath, his face was so close and his soft touch was still on my cheek.

I averted my gaze and backed away.

"It's late, I should go home now."

"Right," he sighed and then gave me that beautiful smile of his that I couldn't look away from. "You can call me at any time, I'm always free."

I walked past him and nodded, not really sure if he even saw it.

I muttered a quiet sure and was ready to leave when I felt a firm grasp on my hands.

Mako had taken off his jacket off and held it in front of me with his other hand. "Wear this."

"I don't need it."

"You're literally barefoot, you should at least wear a jacket," he chuckled but I could see the worry in his eyes. I sighed and grabbed his the jacket.

"Thanks."

I stepped back and put on the jacket and felt myself being soothed by his scent. It somehow calmed my nerves.

Even if I wanted to object I knew he wouldn't let me walk back alone so I didn't say anything when he was a step behind me. Honestly the walk back home wasn't as bad as I thought it would be. It was quiet and calmed my heart, like all my worries had just disappeared. I wanted to keep this feeling forever.

'Strange.'

Chapter 19 - Unusual Days Are A Given Now

F^{emi}

Today had been a stranger day than usual, throughout the whole day Darianna looked like she was one edge and whenever a certain someone would walk past her she'd ease up for a moment. But then tense up right after. And that certain someone was Mako, he didn't seem to have noticed her strange behavior or he was just really good at hiding it. But I did notice how he'd steal quick glances at her and then go back to talking to his friends, something Darianna definitely didn't notice.

Something happened between them. I was sure of it.

I couldn't stop the smirk that crept up on my lips and Darianna frowned once she saw it.

"What?" she asked with a sharp tone.

"Ohhh, nothing.." I muttered as I glanced down with my smirk still on display. "It's just, you seem a bit out of it today. Did something.. special happen lately?"

Darianna's breath hitched and then looked away from me. "What makes you think that?"

I blinked with a innocent gleam in my eyes as I looked at her.

"No reason," I smiled and then dragged her to class.

We sat in the groups that had to do with our essays. Mako was halfway done, Ashton had already finished it— most likely so he'd have more time to do nothing during our lessons—, I was a third way done and Darianna had barely even started.

It didn't even take a second before Mako let out a loud sigh and started getting distracted. "Thinking about going to a party, I don't know if I should go alone this time."

"I'll go with you," I muttered.

The way Ashton and Darianna looked at me made it clear that they weren't really pleased. Ashton was gonna say something but was cut off by Darianna whose voice was shaky.

"Why?" She leaned in closer and whispered into my ear. "Why would you?"

I looked at her without saying anything and it was as if she could read what I was thinking. She sighed and then gave me a small smile.

"Alright.. Just make sure you stick with me or Ashton. Never wander alone."

I nodded and gave her a soft smile, I wasn't gonna make a mistake like that ever again. Just because John was gone didn't mean there weren't several other John's out there, I had to be careful.

Ashton still looked at me with furrowed brows but I ignored it.

"Wait, what makes you think Ashton would go?" I whispered.

Darianna smirked and then poked my forehead. "Why do you think?"

I felt my face heat up but pushed whatever stupid thoughts that would come out down.

"How about you work on the essay instead," I scowled which made Darianna laugh.

.

.

We were at the party and this time I had actually been able to enjoy it. I wasn't drinking or dancing on the floor but the feeling was nice and I spent most of my time with Darianna. Mako had tried to talk to Darianna but whenever he did she'd evade it so eventually he gave up. I mouthed a 'Sorry' once I saw him and he smiled at me and then mouthed back a 'It's okay'.

I wanted to ask Darianna about what was making her act like that towards him, she'd enjoyed being with him those other days and she didn't seem particularly angry at him right now, so what was making her act like that?

We went up to the balcony to get some fresh air and I felt as my whole body cooled down. I hadn't noticed just how hot my body felt. Someone else entered the balcony but I didn't care to look and see who it was, but Darianna did. She stepped back and was ready to leave.

"You're just gonna leave?"

She chuckled and gave me a smirk. Before I could stop she was already out the door. I turned to see who the person she had left me with was and felt my throat get dry once I saw who it was.

"Ashton, why're you here?"

He didn't reply and continued walking and soon stood next to me. The sky light made his skin glimmer with a blue hue and his electric eyes looked as cold as ever.

"Did you maybe.." I whispered. "Come here for me?"

Chapter 20 - Getting Closer Under The Moon

F^{emi}

It was a stupid question, a really stupid question, one which Ashton didn't even bother to answer. "Sorry, nevermind. Just forget I asked that," I sighed.

Ashton still looked at the beautiful view of the midnight sky covered in bright stars and clouds. The ground had some people laying down, most likely drunk but it still looked nice. "Why'd you come here?" Ashton's deep voice sprung me out of my thoughts and I turned to him.

"Why shouldn't I?"

His brows furrowed and he gave me a typical cold glare. "'Why?' Have you already forgotten what happened a few days ago?"

"No," my answer came out as easily as breathing. "How could I ever forget?"

His eyes softened. He let out a weak sigh and looked away for a moment.

"I just don't want to miss out on fun just because of some creeps. I don't want them to have that power over me."

Ashton gave me a soft pat on my head and then smirked. "Seems like you're not that weak crybaby anymore. Never thought you'd change this much."

I couldn't look away from his gaze, it was entrapping.

"Not your crybaby?"

Ashton's smirk got more mischievous. He looked away to the view, "stupid question."

I felt how my heartbeat quickened. How was he always able to make my body react in such strange ways?

"You should be careful with how you speak," I noticed the glance he gave me and I smirked. "Any girl would think you're into them if you act like that. Or maybe, is it actually like that?"

Ashton chuckled and then leaned in. "And what would you do if it was?"

My heart skipped a beat but I hid the effects his words had on me. "I'd turn you down of course, I've never seen you that way."

His smirk grew wider and he leaned in even closer, to the point where our lips nearly touched. His warm breath tickled my lips and I closed my eyes by instinct.

But our lips never met.

I stayed still for a moment.

And when I opened my eyes he was looking out again.

I could hear his chuckle and my face went warm.

'How could he do something like that?'

I looked back out at the view and hid just how flushed my face had become. My heart was still beating like crazy but if I just stayed calm for a moment it would've calmed down, eventually.

I took a quick glance at Ashton and wondered if this had effected him too.

Had his heart quickened?

Even just a little bit?

.

.

Darianna had been even stranger than usual at school, she rarely answered when I talked to her and it looked like her head was somewhere else. We sat on top of the staircase, the one few students rarely used, and ate some snacks.

Well it was mainly me, she'd just take a bite out of her chips every few minutes while starring at nothing in a daze.

I'd never seen her like this from all the years I had known her.

"We should probably get to class, Ashton and Mako are probably waiting."

Darianna sprung up at my words and her face flushed. "Mako.." she whispered quietly, more to herself than me.

"Yes Mako." I eyed her carefully and then smiled. "Do you.. like him?"

She turned to me with wide eyes and gripped her chips so tightly I wondered if the chips were even intact anymore.

"I would never-"

"Right," I smirked.

I got up and skipped down the stairs as I heard Darianna fumbling with her belongings as she ran down the stairs.

"Girl don't even," she glared at me and that only made me laugh more.

Her dark skin made it hard, but if I looked closely there was a tint that showed that she was blushing.

'Seems like my best friend has finally fallen in love.'

Chapter 21 - They're Just Strange Acquaintances

D arianna

Now what the hell was all that about? I shouldn't have listened but for some reason I still did something I knew I'd regret. He asked me for a dance and for some reason I said yes.

It was only supposed to be a dance yet the way he looked at me, that hungry gaze, I froze up. And once he leaned in I nearly let him kiss me. I had to back away and leave, I couldn't do that. Maybe I should've just stayed with Femi instead. That balcony was nice. But then again, staying meant also being stuck with Ashton and that was a definite no.

I took out my phone and gave Femi a quick text saying I had to leave and she answered in about a second. Worrying of course, asking if I'm alright so I had to reassure her that I really was okay.

I sat on a bench near a park and looked at the sky instead of going home. If I waited a little longer he would've been asleep and then I could go. But for now I just let the warm breeze tickly my skin as I listened the rustling of the leaves.

Femi had been pestering me all morning about my "supposed" crush on Mako which was one of the dumbest things I'd ever heard.

She really mistook my behaviour for me liking him. I just didn't feel like being near him that's all. He'd seen me cry, something even Femi hadn't and heard bits about my homelife. I couldn't feel comfortable knowing that he'd seen so much about me. It was a suffocating feeling.

But also I just felt strange, whenever I was near him my heart would be at ease and for some reason I always wanted to stay by his side a little longer. It was strange, so strange and I hated it.

I didn't have a crush nor was I in love, I was just acting a bit out of it. Just hadn't slept enough, 'yeah that's all'.

Femi wrapped her arm around me and looked at me with expectant eyes.

"You sure you don't like someone?" She giggled.

"God you're so annoying."

Her grin grew wider and I just wanted to wipe that smug face off her mouth.

"Maybe we should focus on your love life instead." I smiled and Femi gave me a confused look. "Y'know, you and Ashton. What happened to you hating him? Doesn't seem that way too me anymore."

She backed away from me and her eyes went wide. I could tell how flustered she'd become and I smirked.

"Me and Ashton are not like that! We're barely even friends, just strange acquaintances?" It sounded like Femi became more unsure by the end and I hummed.

"Ohhh, I see. Sure, sure."

Femi's brows knitted together and she huffed which caused me to chuckle. She was such an easy person to read.

She let out a sigh then gave me a soft smile. "It's just nice seeing you like this, you've dated several times before but you never had such a glow when you were with them." Her voice went quiet, "sometimes I wondered if it all changed because of E-"

"Thanks Femi. Really, but I'm honestly not into anyone right now. Love has never really been my thing."

Femi eyed me for a moment and her eyes went droopy. She gave me a slow nod.

I let out a sigh and gave her a small smile. "Well, guess who finally got a parttime job."

Her eyes lit up and she looked at me with a bright smile.

"You got a job? Nice!"

"Yup, can't wait to get my money," I smirked and Femi giggled.

"Good for you, I'm not even gonna bother applying for jobs," she sighed. "By the way what job did you get?"

"Oh, just the convenience store near that really big hotel."

"Ah nice, maybe I'll visit you." She smiled but I bumped her shoulder.

"Girl, you'd be distracting. Don't even."

She laughed and wrapped her arm around mine as we walked to class together.

My first shift would start today after school and hopefully it wouldn't go too badly.

Chapter 22 - Missing Out On Everything

D arianna

So about this not going too badly, of course that couldn't happen. Everything had gone okay in the beginning, there weren't that many customers and it was pretty easy to navigate the store. But once the sun had set and I looked out I noticed a familiar pair of green eyes staring at me.

I ignored it at first, could've just been anyone, but when he entered the store and gave me that creepy smile he always did— I knew it was him.

He bought a bottle of strawberry milk and then left the store, but I could still see him outside, his eyes glued to me.

My shift ended but I still stayed in the store. I couldn't go out alone.

'Maybe I should call Femi?'

'No, he won't be scared off by a girl like her. And he may do something to her..'

'Then who?'

'Ah.'

My breathing quickened but I tried to keep it steady. There was no one else I could call. He was the only one.

.

.

I heard the familiar ping and pulled up my phone to scan it for any signs that I'd just gotten a message. Which I had.

I felt how all the stress left my shoulders once I saw his text.

"I'm outside."

I got up and crept through the door and even from here I could see that he was still standing there, at that same spot. But this time he was calmly scrolling through his phone.

My body didn't want to move after seeing him, I'd frozen again, but once I saw— just a glimpse— of Mako standing at the other side I felt my breathing calm. His dark brown hair a bit ruffled and his sun kissed skin seemed a bit wet. Was he sweaty? Had he ran here?

Well the message I sent him was just a simple 'help' and some info about where I was. I would've been pretty worried too if I were in his position.

I stepped out of the store and before Ethan could react and talk to me I grabbed Mako's hand and gave him a smile. "Thanks for waiting."

"Who is that Dari?" the creep asked and I turned around, giving him a nonchalant gaze.

"My boyfriend. Why?" My grip tightened on Mako's hand to make sure he wouldn't say anything unnecessary. He seemed to have understood as he pulled me closer to him and wrapped one arm around me. 'Okay, this may be a bit overkill..'

Ethan looked like he wanted to say something more but choked on his words and turned around, his face flushed red. What did I ever see in him?

Ethan had been my boyfriend but after his continuous cheating I had to break it off, and I found out he was cheating in the worst way possible.

I didn't want to deal with him alone since while he was short and skinny he was still pretty aggressive and would have some problems with his anger. I was lucky that he never raised a hand on me.

I needed someone who could scare him off, preferably a man but I didn't really have many male friends who fit the bill. Except Mako, he was fairly tall, was pretty well built and had sharp features. A weakling like Ethan would feel intimidated just from looking at him.

I stepped out of Mako's grasp and muttered a quiet sorry. He shrugged, "it's okay," he said. I couldn't tell whether he wanted to know more or not.

"Aren't you interested? You've seen some pretty strange things about me but never asked about any of them. Most would ask me about who that guy was or something like that."

"I am interested."

I looked up at him and blinked, I was honestly caught of guard by his words.

"But I don't want to force you into a position where you have to tell me," Mako said as he looked into the blinding convenience store, his eyes squinting a bit.

"Oh."

Without thinking my body leaned in and I kissed him, well it was just a peck. My eyes went wide once I'd realized what I'd just done and I pulled back. My gaze stayed to the ground so I couldn't tell how he was looking at me.

"Sorry! Sorry, I wasn't thinking!"

"Do you regret it?" His voice was quiet and deep, as smooth as velvet and it made my ears perk up.

"No," my voice came out in a low and breathless tone.

He pulled me into him and pressed his lips onto mine. I wrapped my arms around him and leaned into his kiss. I couldn't breath and the only thing I could hear was my loud heartbeat thumping in my ear.

I pulled back, my body breathless and I looked into his piercing black eyes— ones I could get lost in forever.

"My father.. he's a piece of shit who never knows when to shut up, and that guy from before, he's my ex," Mako's grip tightened after my use of the word 'ex'. "That guy has way too many faults too list," I sighed.

"Love has never been something I was good at, I never really had great examples so I guess I was too scared to ever really try it out."

"But it's different when I'm with you, I don't want to miss out on everything anymore just 'cause I'm scared."

I burrowed my head into his chest and breathed out a quiet, "I like you."

Chapter 23 - A Thin Towel Doesn't Cover Much

F emi

I got out of the shower and sat down on my bed, I was ready to put on my pajamas when I heard a low ping from my phone. So I picked it up and was hit with bright light, I lowered the brightness and looked to see what the notification was for.

"you're right I do like someone"

"i kissed him lol"

"and he kissed me back omfg??"

"its Mako btw"

"bye, gonna go sleep now"

My eyes kept on getting wider as I read her messages. Darianna was actually into someone this time? And not dating just to waste time? Oh, I had to hear all about this at school.

A high pitched shriek escaped my lips as I plopped down onto the bed, laughing in joy. Darianna was my best friend and was the kindest person I knew, but I could always feel a weird sorrowful feeling from her. But there was nothing I could do about it so I'd tried to be by her side at least.

Hearing her have something to gush about, something to be fully happy about filled me with ease. Nearly to the point of my stupid tears but I wiped them before they could come.

A knock came from downstairs so I got up and went down. It couldn't be my parents, they were never home at this time so maybe it was Ashton? But why would he have come here at this time of day.

I opened the door and Ashton stood there, his black hair a bit damp— I could see his eyebrow piercing peek through his hair— and he frowned as he looked at me.

"What was that scream about?"

"Scream? Oh, sorry I just heard some good news and couldn't hold in my emotions."

He sighed and then gave me a glare, "don't scream like that over something so stupid, had me all worried."

'Oh?'

I took a step closer to him and looked into his eyes with a smirk. "Worried?"

His eyebrows knitted even closer together and he was gonna reply but stopped at his tracks. His eyes travelled down my body and that's when I realized that I had forgotten to put on my clothes. I was just in a thin, small, white towel. In front of him of all people.

I staggered back and shut the door so hard a loud slam echoed throughout my empty house. "Sorry!" was all I could say before I ran up the stairs to put on my clothes.

.

.

School had been exceptionally fun today. I bombarded Darianna with questions and while she'd scoff I could see the way her eyes lit up whenever she talked about him.

We'd also finished the essay so I didn't have to think about that anymore, we'd all gotten our parts done and handed it in.

There was only one problem with today though, I'd caught a nasty cold and at first it was just an annoying headache. But as the hours passed my breathing became rugged— if I could even breath at all— my body started to heat up and my sight went dizzy.

I would've just gone home if it weren't for the fact that in the second to last lesson we were gonna have a pretty big test and I preferred to get if done sooner rather than later.

Only a few more lessons and then I could go home. Just a few more.

Chapter 24 - It's A Simple Truth

Ashton

Something bumped into me and muttered a weak sorry. I turned around too see Femi standing behind me, breathless and barely standing. She didn't even have the strength to look up at me.

She tried to walk past me but lost her footing and fell on me but I grabbed her by the shoulder.

"Why're you in school?" I asked.

"For the test." She breathed out. "I can go home now.." Her speech was slow and slurred, to the point where it looked like she was dozing off.

"Alone? Like this?" I sighed and gripped her hand and pulled her out of the school.

"What're you doing?" She turned around, watching as the school got smaller.

"You said you wanted to get home right?"

"Yes but why're you coming with me? Don't you have classes?"

She always asked stupid questions. I stayed quiet and continued walking with her behind me. Just from holding her hand I could feel how much her body was burning up. To the point I questioned how she'd even survived so much of the school day.

Femi muttered a quiet sorry and stopped asking questions. All I could hear from her were her staggered breathing.

.

.

We got to her home and it had a chilling air to it. The whole house was dark, being only lit up by the lights from outside. "Is your home always this cold?"

She nodded and went up the stairs as she held the wall for support.

I'd never noticed it before but Femi's parents were rarely ever at home were they? She never really talked about them and didn't seem to worry about bringing a guy to her home to clean his wounds up. Most girls would've worried about how their parents would've reacted if they found out.

Even during kindergarten, did her parents ever show up during any of the parental meetings?

"Ashton." Her soft voice broke me out of my thoughts and I realized we were standing in her room. It was pretty clean and organized, something I would've expected from her. "Are you gonna stay forever or? Shouldn't you get back to school?"

I shrugged my shoulders and looked around in her room with earned me a frown from her. She didn't really come off as threatening, more like a cute hamster.

"Are you gonna call your parents? You're pretty sick and they're doctors right? They could help you out."

She looked at me in a daze and blinked. "Why would I— Oh.. no, it's alright. The cold isn't that bad." She sat down on her bed and turned away from me, looking out the window.

Her voice came out in a low whisper but I still heard it. "Doubt they'd care."

I felt a quick but sharp pain in my heart. Had she grown up like this? All alone? Was her life always like this?

It filled me with a feeling of guilt, after all I bullied her and made her already tiresome life worse.

For several reasons, but one of them was how I thought her life was easier than mine. But I didn't understand her as much as I'd thought.

I sat down next to her bed and she twitched but still looked away from me.

"I could stay."

A sharp inhale could be heard. She shook her head and chuckled.

"No, you need to get back to class. Your mom will worry if you don't."

"Right," I groaned and got up. She looked at me for a moment and then looked down.

"Ashton."

"Yeah?" I had gotten to the door but stopped.

"Why did you," she sighed. "Why did you bully me?"

I remained silent and heard how the bed creaked. She was looking at me now.

"I deserve to know." Her voice while weak was still sharp. It must've come out in a harsher tone than she'd intended as she sighed right after. "Why?"

"Because." I looked back at her. "I was jealous."

I closed the door and walked out.

I doubt she even understood what I meant but it was as simple as that.

I'd been jealous of her. And reacted to it in a horrible way.

One that hurt her.

Chapter 25 - Pent Up Emotions Never End Well

A shton

My childhood hadn't exactly been the best. I was around seven when it all started. The usual bickering turned into full on shouting matches and sometimes even blood would be spilled. I saw it all but had to stay quiet. And after everything they decided to get a divorce.

The process was slow and painful, it dragged on forever, like time wasn't passing.

Glances would be sent my way, ones of pity, scorn and sometimes even mock. But it didn't bother me. I just didn't want them to look at me like I was some zoo animal. I wasn't some exhibition they could sit back and enjoy. But I kept it all in.

I couldn't show how I felt.

My mother was already too busy having to deal with her job, the paperwork and my father. To the point where she forgot to deal with me.

I still remember the way she looked at me when I told her I needed help with my homework. It was a lie, I knew how to answer it all but just wanted to spend a little time with her. But her expression shut me up.

A look that said, 'another thing to deal with? I can't do this anymore.' She looked like she was gonna curl up and cry at any moment. So I lied and told her it was okay. I gave her a smile and went to my room. If she couldn't see me then it'd be easier to forget I exist. Then I wouldn't be a bother to her anymore. That's what I'd thought.

Whenever I got to school I'd see the same girl crying. It was always over something stupid, like a small cut, a spilled drink or someone raised their voice.

Her tears irritated me.

I hated it.

I hated her.

So I made sure she knew.

But as I got older I realized how I really felt. I didn't hate her. I was just jealous.

I had so many pent up emotions and never got the chance to show them but she was able to do it so easily. I wanted what she had and didn't know how to react to it so I mocked her for her crying, teased her and annoyed her until she avoided even being in the same room as me. Never looking at me and tensing up whenever we walked past each other.

It was stupid, I was stupid.

I regretted it all yet whenever she looked at me it wasn't filled with the hate I'd expected from her. Instead she smiled my way, like I deserved to see it.

That's why I wanted to distance myself from her. I thought that was what she needed best. But she didn't seem to agree. She kept on trying to get closer, and now I was too used to having her in my life to go back to how it was before.

No apologies would ever take back from the way I hurt her, the past couldn't be changed.

That's why I'd sworn to never hurt her and make sure that she was always smiling.

She was always prettiest when she smiled.

I'd always thought that,

even back then.

A/N

Making things clear even though he thought she was prettiest when she smiled when they were kids he did not have a crush on her then

I don't want to make this into one of those weird "he bullied you cus he likes you" situations lmao

Also this chapter isn't meant to make his bullying okay, just wanted to explain it and show from his perspective how it turned out that way

Chapter 26 - Everybody Loves Cute Plushies

Femi

The look on Ashton's face was till stuck on my mind. When he told me why he bullied me, he had a sorrowful expression. His eyes were dark, like they were filled with regret.

And his words.

"I was jealous."

Jealous? Of who? Me?

I wanted to ask but at the same time I didn't. Like I had learned enough, I was content with what I knew. Sometimes things were simpler than what they seemed.

My cool pillow cooled my burning body. I pressed into it and let myself wander into sleep.

.

.

The sound of a distant knock made my eyes flutter open. Someone was knocking downstairs. And my body rose from the bed, still slow from my cold.

My sleep had fixed me up a bit though, I wasn't as exhausted from before.

I went down the stairs as cool air passed my body and got to the door. I opened it and was met with glimmering light brown eyes looking at me. Darianna stood at the other side with a smile and a bag in one hand.

"What're you doing here?" I managed to say, my voice raspy and slow. She cocked a smile and raised a brow.

"Girl have you forgotten what day it is?"

I stared at her in silence and she laughed.

"It's your birthday girl. That cold really took a lot out of you huh?" She laughed and I sighed. Of course it was my birthday. I'd completely forgotten and to my defense when you have parents who're to busy to bring it up, your birthday turns into just another day.

I stepped back so she could get in and she leaned in. "I got you a pretty good present."

Mako stood at the back and waved at me. I'd barely even noticed him from how dim the light was outside. But my eyes shot to who stood next to him. Ashton.

I felt how my heartbeat quickened at the sight.

Did I always feel this way when I looked at him?

I averted my gaze and turned around. "You guys can get in, I'm gonna go change."

I went up the stairs and changed out of my trashy pajamas that I'd some-how managed to get on yesterday even through my cold. And put on a simple shirt and sweatpants.

I went downstairs and saw how they had decorated the place in such a short amount of time. The dining room table had several different foods, mainly take outs, all over it and a large strawberry cake in the middle. Strawberry had always been my favorite fruit. Darianna must've picked it.

I smiled and sat down on the couch, next to Mako.

"So what're we gonna do?" I looked at Darianna, "I don't want too loud music playing, I'm still kinda sick."

She rolled her eyes and turned on the tv. "Yeah, yeah. No need to tell me. You're the birthday girl for today."

I chuckled and nudged Mako on the shoulder. He looked at me with a raised brow and I smirked. "So you were able to get Darianna's attention huh?"

His cheeks turned a soft pink and he smiled. "Don't know how I even managed to do it. That girl sure is something else." He sighed out as he looked at her with dreamy eyes. I giggled and was gonna say more when Ashton sat down next to me with a present in hand.

I looked at the blue wrapped present with a dumbfounded expression and spoke. "Is this for me?"

"Who else would it be for?"

"Still got attitude. Even during my birthday." I grumbled and his eyes sharpened.

"Got a problem?"

"Nope," I said as I played with my fingers and then gave him a smirk. "Somehow grew to like this side of you."

His lips parted and then he looked away and put the present on my thighs. "Can I open it?"

"Do whatever you want."

I inspected the present and how neatly it had been wrapped, with such care and precision.

The present was a plushie, about medium sized, of a light blue hamster. My heart melted at the sight. It was the cutest thing I had ever seen and I was fighting off the urge to give it a tight huge right there.

"Thank you." I breathed out with teary eyes.

He stayed silent.

But from the corner of his lips I could see a smile.

Chapter 27 - Always Will Be His Crybaby

F emi

Darianna was watching us with an amused expression. Her eyes shimmered. They had a glint that meant she had plans. Ideas that meant trouble.

"So.." Darianna hummed and I raised a brow. "Since it's your birthday.."

"Yeah?" I replied, agitated from the way she was dragging this out.

"You'll meet Tyler right? It's been a while since you two hung out."

"Oh! Tyler." A large smile appeared on my face and Ashton glanced my way. "I haven't seen him in a while but he always visits during my birthdays. I've got to leave my schedule open."

Darianna picked up a bowl of red grapes and plopped one in her mouth. "Do you have any plans for what you'll do?"

"No, don't think so. He's usually the one who decides. I just follow along."
I giggled and for a second there I could've sworn I just saw Ashton grip the
wrapping from the present.

"Who's Tyler?" Ashton asked, his gray eyes were filled with an emotion I'd
never seen from him before.

"Oh he's just my—"

"He's someone Femi grew up with." Darianna cut in. "She mentioned him
to me recently, he's probably the second closest person to her, right after
me." She smirked and Ashton raised a brow.

Mako took the controller Darianna had put down a few moments before
and started scrolling through the channels. "Great. We can talk about that
Tyler guy another day. Right now we should be partying."

Darianna shot him an annoyed glare and he gave her a smirk. He turned to
me. "Do you have Netflix?"

I nodded and he smiled. "Great."

"Let her decide what we should watch." Darianna crossed her arms and
Mako rolled her eyes.

"I was just about to ask."

"Mhmm, sure."

"So what do you want to watch?" Mako made sure to emphasize the 'you'
and I couldn't help but smile.

"Well how about... Stranger things? Or Riverdale? We could laugh at how
bad it is."

Mako searched for Riverdale and laughed. "Great choice."

Darianna sat down at one of the small sofas that was in front of the dining table and smiled. "This is gonna be a long night."

And she was right. It was definitely a long night of laughing screaming and partying. We watched trashy shows, Passionflix movies and then horror movies that had me gripping my plushie. Ashton had placed his hand on mine but that just distracted me from the movie to him.

It was probably one of the nicest birthdays I had had in a while.

I'd gotten a adorable plushie from Ashton, a silver heart necklace from Mako and a set of golden and silver jewels I could add to my box braids next time from Darianna. All the dear presents I'd gotten were placed in my room near my shelf.

I wanted this day to last forever.

.

.

Mako and Darianna had left as Ashton stayed with me in the kitchen. The house was pretty clean even after everything that'd happened. I'd offered to help with the cleaning but they'd shut me down. Saying that since it was my birthday I only needed to sit back. Also because I still had a cold.

I took a glass of water and eyed Ashton who was scrolling through his phone. He put it down and walked to me.

"Do you like Tyler?"

"What?!" My voice nearly came out as a scream from the unexpectedness of the question. "I- I mean what..? Why would you ask that?"

His brows furrowed and he inched closer to me. "Your face immediately changed once he got brought up. Looked like you really like him."

"And what if I do?"

He leaned in and kissed me. My body froze up and my eyes went wide. His kiss was filled with hunger and longing and I returned it. He pulled back, his lips just inches from mine and his breath tickling my skin. "I won't let you."

Darianna is gonna go crazy once she hears about this.

I smirked and looked into his eyes. "Tyler is my cousin."

Silence feel between us.

"Oh."

I chuckled and kissed him. My body wanted this, needed this. I couldn't tell when the change happened but along the way I'd wanted to become his. And he seemed to have felt the same way. As he grabbed my hips and pushed my body into his and placed kisses over my neck.

Like he was marking it, removing any signs that John had been there.

I pulled back, gasping for air and let out a laugh. I couldn't hold it in. "I can't believe it, you really were jealo—"

He shut me up with a kiss and through rugged breathes I heard him breathe out a 'you're mine' and that made me lean into him even more.

I really was his.